SUNNY
MAKES A SPLASH

JENNIFER L. HOLM & MATTHEW HOLM
WITH COLOR BY LARK PIEN

graphix
AN IMPRINT OF
SCHOLASTIC

Library of Congress data available

ISBN 978-1-338-23318-6 (hardcover)
ISBN 978-1-338-23317-9 (paperback)

10 9 8 7 6 5 4 3 2 1   21 22 23 24 25

Printed in China 62
First edition, September 2021
Edited by David Levithan
Lettering by Fawn Lau
Color by Lark Pien
Creative Director: Phil Falco
Publisher: David Saylor

For Jo

Thanks for the Memories!

SPRING FLING!

TOUCH DOWN!

BRAVO!

The **VOTES** are in...
Here are our favorites!

FRIENDLIEST

Brian

BEST HAIR

Deb

COOLEST GUY

Rob

SMARTEST

Arun

CLASS CLOWN

Dwayne

COOLEST GIRL

Lisa

**MOST LIKELY
TO SUCCEED**

BEST COUPLE

Tony

Larry and Mary

CHAPTER TWO:
Keep Cool

PANT   PANT

SKIDDDDDDD

Aaaah.

15

16

CHAPTER THREE:
Splash

21

25

1970s POOL!

CRAZY HIGH SLIDE!

DEEP END IS SIXTEEN FEET DEEP!

CRAZY HIGH DIVING BOARD!

THE 1970s WERE CRAZY!

Gulp.

STARSKY & HUTCH

Your favorite show is on, Sunny!

Sunset

STARSKY & HUTCH

POPULAR TV SHOW ABOUT TWO COPS

STARSKY!
(BRUNETTE)

HUTCH!
(BLOND)

THEY DRIVE A
RED CAR CALLED
"THE STRIPED
TOMATO."

THEY ARE
BEST BUDDIES
AND MAKE
WISECRACKS.

CHAPTER FIVE:
Snack Bar

48

53

CHAPTER SIX:
Hot Dog Tongs

56

57

CHAPTER SEVEN:
Don't Run

Don't run!

SLIP!

WHAM!

WINCE

Oof.

Waaahhhhhh!!!

Hey, Sunny, can you pass me the first aid kit?

Waahh ...

CHAPTER EIGHT:
T-shirt

75

CHAPTER NINE:
Roof Fell In

84

85

CHAPTER TEN:
Drama

100

Hey, old girl.
How was
your day?

Way too
much drama.

978 **Philadelphia Bulletin** 15-D

Weather Summary

TODAY'S FORECAST
Hot with chance of afternoon showers

REGION

	High	Low
Allentown	72	53
Atlantic City	74	66
Harrisburg	75	63
Philadelphia	80	67
Pittsburgh	74	53
Scranton	72	53
Wilmington	78	65

New Moon	1st Qtr.	Full Moon	3rd Qtr.
JULY 5	JULY 13	JULY 19	JULY 26

SUN AND MOON
Sun sets .... 8:31 p.m.
Sun rises .... 5:42 a.m.
Moon sets .... 11:31 p.m.

NATION   SKY CONDITIONS

CRUNCH

Well?
Is it good?

The Nutty
Buddy was
better.

Tony, why
won't your dad
just let us go
home?

There's
no one
here.

You know
how he is. If it
stops raining,
people might
come back?

SPLASH! SPLASH!

There's something in your hair.

There is?

SHOVE!

SPLASH!

He's totally fallen for you!

CHAPTER THIRTEEN:
Salad Bar

144

CHAPTER FOURTEEN:
Sherbet

I've never understood sherbet.

It's so confusing!

It is?

Later that night.

Dad! Do you have any idea what time it is?

BLINK!

I've been waiting up for you!

FLUMP

150

CHAPTER SIXTEEN:
Postcards

PLUM LAKE

Air view of **PLUM LAKE** noted for its fine resorts and housekeeping cottages. A favorite spot for vacationers with its beautiful sandy beaches and excellent walleye and muskie fishing.

I AM SO BORED! SAVE ME! —Deb

p.s. Please write a long letter about how bored you are, too.

I miss you!!!

POST CARD

Sunny Le
1026 Lo
Audubo

HA HA HA!

That night.

Dear Deb,

Dear Deb,
    I got a job at the pool club. Remember Tony from history class? His dad runs the club. It's actually kind of fun.

Two of the lifeguards are Jay and Dawn.

Jay 🤍🤍 Dawn

Jay likes Dawn, but Dawn isn't sure if she likes Jay. But another lifeguard, Pam, maybe also liked Jay (at first)

? Pam

but she is friends with Dawn and thinks that Dawn should date Jay.

It's a real life soap opera! If it was on TV it would be called:

Pool Club Days

Love,
Sunny

The next morning.

Mom!

Where are the stamps?

Try your grandfather's room. He had them last.

"Sweet Myrtle"

You came so softly along the way,
I scarce heard your footsteps fall.
'Twas oh so good we met that day,
Now joined, we stroll along life's hall.

I hear your laughter fill the air,
And listen for your song.
The shining day is oh so fair,
Because you came along.

The next morning.

What's going on? Why's she so mad?

Your mother's just upset because we're both growing up and don't need her as much.

Don't worry. It'll be fine.

Do you like sherbet?

Can't stand the stuff.

DING-DONG!

See you later!

Do you have a sweater?

Yes!

Do you have a dime in case you need to call?

Yep!

Do you have—

Yes!

1970s CANDY!

REGGIE BAR
(NAMED AFTER BASEBALL PLAYER REGGIE JACKSON!)

GOBSTOPPERS
(THEY LAST FOREVER!)

JUJUBES
(SUPER STICKY! TASTE KIND OF LIKE SOAP!)

RAZZLES
(FIRST IT'S CANDY, THEN IT'S GUM!)

GOOD AND PLENTY
(NEITHER GOOD NOR PLENTY)

The next day.

RIIIIIIIINNNGGG!!!

The next day.

Hey, Starsky!

Hutch!

ACKNOWLEDGMENTS

We had many lifeguards who helped Sunny make her splash! Many thanks to our hardworking crew: Lark Pien and Fawn Lau. The gang at Graphix kept us in top form, especially David Levithan, Phil Falco, and Lauren Donovan. As always, thanks to Cyndi Koon and our lovely agent Jill Grinberg.

Finally, we owe a debt of gratitude to our late grandfather, Michael Hearn, who wrote the poem "Sweet Myrtle." He had the heart of a romantic and the soul of a poet.

A NOTE FROM JENNIFER L. HOLM & MATTHEW HOLM

Sunny's summer adventure was inspired by Jenni's childhood. Her first real job (after babysitting) was working at the snack bar of the local pool. She handed out ice cream and sodas and was a whiz at deep-frying french fries. Eventually, she became a lifeguard at the same pool and spent far too much time telling kids not to run. To this day, if she sees a kid running around a pool, she will shout at them to walk. (Falling on wet concrete is no joke!)

JENNIFER L. HOLM & MATTHEW HOLM are the award-winning brother-sister team behind the Babymouse and Squish series. Jennifer is also the author of many acclaimed novels, including three Newbery Honor books and the NEW YORK TIMES bestseller THE FOURTEENTH GOLDFISH.

LARK PIEN, the colorist of SUNNY MAKES A SPLASH, is an indie cartoonist from Oakland, California. She has published many comics and is the colorist for Printz Award winner AMERICAN BORN CHINESE and BOXERS & SAINTS. Her characters Long Tail Kitty and Mr. Elephanter have been adapted into children's books. You can follow her on Twitter @larkpien.